Sonia Edwards is originally from Cemaes in Anglesey. *A White Veil for Tomorrow* won the Prose Medal at the National Eisteddfod in 1999. She has published two other collections of short stories – *Glas Ydi'r Nefoedd* and *Gloynnod* which won Welsh Book of the Year in 1996. She has also published four novels *Cysgu Ar Eithin* (1994), *Llen Dros yr Haul* (1997), *Cadwyn o Flodau* (2000) and *Cywion Uffern* (2000). In 1998 she published a volume of poetry *Y Llais yn y Llun*.

She lives and works in Llangefni where she teaches Welsh.

PARTHIAN BOOKS

A White Veil for Tomorrow

Sonia Edwards

PARTHIAN BOOKS

Parthian Books
53 Colum Road
Cardiff
CF10 3EF
www.parthianbooks.co.uk

This translation first published in 2001.
All rights reserved.
Translation © Sonia Edwards 2001.
ISBN 1-902638-17-4

A White Veil for Tomorrow was originally published as
Rhwng Noson Wen A Phlygain by Gwasg Gwynedd in
1999.

This book has been translated from the Welsh by
Sonia Edwards.

Typeset by NW.

Printed and bound by Colourbooks, Dublin.

The publishers would like to thank the Arts Council of
Wales for support in the translation and publication of
this book.

Parthian would also like to thank Alwena Owen and
everyone at Gwasg Gwynedd for cooperation in the
organisation of the translation.

With support from the Parthian Collective.

Cover design and photograph by Joe Mazelis.

A CIP catalogue record for this book is available from
the British Library.

Stories

IN MEMORY
OF
MAIR

But I, being poor, have only my dreams;
I have spread my dreams under your feet;
Tread softly because you tread on my dreams.

A White Veil For Tomorrow

A virgin's hands. Small. White. Lilies and clover and the smiles of nuns. And Gwyneth herself. Dear fair-skinned Gwyneth, a woman with a young girl's tresses.

And Gwyneth looked down at her lily-white hands as if she were searching for a blemish, a stain. Anything that shouldn't have been there. It was as if she could not believe in their purity.

"I've got a boyfriend, you know," she said. I heard little chimes of wonderment rippling under her voice.

She raised her eyes, waiting for my response. But I didn't know how to congratulate her. How to look into her innocence without blushing. Until I saw the secret within her smile - a little pool of light like a buttercup's shadow.

"Have you, my pet?"

"Yes, I tell you!" And that familiar 'I tell you!' drew us closer, back to the remains of all our summers and the smell of the earth ripening.

"Don't tell, will you, Deio Bach?"

Even though I'm the eldest. The big brother. And she was the only one who ever got to call me 'Little Deio'.

"Don't tell who? Dad?"

"No one!"

White curls of wood-smoke from a bygone autumn clouded my mind's eye . . . .

What're you up to, Deio Ba-ach? Caught you no-ow! So I ha-ave! Deio Ba-ach kissing girls! Wait till Dad finds out . . . . Flushed cheeks, sweaty palms - No, Gwyneth, don't tell; taunting - crying - leaves a-crackling - Gwyneth, don't you dare, mustn't tell . . . . a fall: blood-and-tears - kiss-away-your-fears . . . . No, Deio Bach, Gwyneth won't tell . . . .

"No, Gwyneth. I won't tell if that's what you want."

She was the one in control of everything while my own faith in things became a trickling of sand between my fingers. She thanked me with her eyes, the brush of her hand against my arm. I doubted whether she knew how attractive and flirtatious she became when she behaved like that. Her body language gave her so much power, and yet so much fragility. I felt a burst of brotherly love towards her and those moments were ever so nearly beautiful.

"Who is he, then?"

That's what ruined everything. Me and my suspicions and my big, careless mouth. And I stood guilty in the face of her happiness thinking all these bitter thoughts about who he might be, this unscrupulous bastard who was taking advantage of her sweetness.

"You don't have to worry, you know, Deio. He's special."

She read the tension that was tightening the muscles in my face as if I were being controlled by a puppeteer's strings. "We're proper lovers." And she smiled without a trace of malice. "Like you and Cadi used to be."

I never knew that anyone suspected Cadi and me. And now I found that Gwyneth, of all people, had made herself a part of our secret all those years ago. The look in her eyes brought a tingling nostalgia in its wake. That night was so easy to remember. It's so easy still, remembering. Too easy. Maybe I don't really want to forget. Maybe that's the clean-picked bare-boned truth of it all. Not wanting to forget a thundery night and Gwyneth in tears. A night in gloved-fingers, deceitful, exquisite and its guilt all bitter-sweet. And I wanted to remember it in all its black darkness because Cadi was part of it . . . .

* * * * * * * * * * * * * * * * *

"Don't go, Deio."

It was humid and stifling and that July sulked to an end, still pressing its heat into the remains of the day. A storm brewed somewhere far off. The sky waited, ready to break. Like her eyes.

"Please, Deio Bach. Don't leave me on my own."

I could do nothing but turn on her. Lose my temper. Stifle my guilt.

"Don't be a baby, Gwyneth! Come on, for God's sake! You're a big girl now . . . "

But she wasn't, was she? Her fifteen years weren't like everyone else's. I chose not to think about that. It was easier to look at her and see a young girl almost as tall as I was, her body graceful and healthy; that's how I wanted to see her because I couldn't cope with her innocence that night. She had no right to force it upon me. And I was thankful for the extreme humidity pressing its heat deeper, deeper into my conscience.

"Dad would be mad at you . . . . you promised . . . . I want Dad to come home . . . "

The cracks between her words were like twigs snapping, betraying the little girl who lived inside her head.

"Please, Gwyneth . . . . don't get upset . . .he'll be back tomorrow. Don't now, Gwyn . . . . . "

She opened up her face to this sham of tenderness and I hated myself for using it only to persuade her.

"Deio, must you go out?"

I held her, drew her close so that I didn't have to look into her eyes. Because Cadi's eyes were somewhere inside me, scanning my shame, and I longed for her until it hurt.

"I won't be late, Gwyn. I promise."

"Really truly promise?"

"Really truly promise."

And the sky was the colour of her tearstains, pressing against the windows. Everything felt swollen and still as if the whole universe were about to burst.

"I'll go to bed and listen out for you. Alright?"

"Alright."

"Listen for the key-turning-in-the-lock sound, alright?"

"Yes, alright."

"It'll be you there then, won't it?"

"Yes, it'll be me there!"

In spite of myself I couldn't keep my voice steady. I knew that she'd noticed the tension that was holding my words together because she lowered her eyelids at that last exclamation mark, almost as if she were reading me on paper, and I thought of her then as a big expensive doll with cry-baby eyes. But she didn't cry, just bent down to stroke the cat that was rubbing itself against her ankles.

"Right, then," she said, without looking up. Her words, like her stance, shimmered with her child-like courage. Had she lifted her eyes then I would have stayed. But she didn't. And with that 'right, then' of hers, I went out without bothering to look back and wave at her as I would normally have done - she wouldn't have come to stand on the doorstep to watch me go that night.

It had started to rain before I arrived at the minister's house, great lumps of it falling aimlessly as if a necklace had broken above my head. That's what made me hurry then because although I yearned to be with Cadi the guilt of having left Gwyneth alone had become like treacle under the soles of my feet. Cadi was there opening the door before I'd even reached the house, ensnaring me as she always did with that shy first-smile-of-the-evening, drawing my need towards her. She had a knack of doing that, of perfecting a new-minted-shyness to woo me anew each time. And yet, the minute I saw her, I knew that tonight would be no ordinary night. I can still remember that stagnant cold as I stepped into the house, a coldness tinged with the dignity of a minister's house, a coldness which was almost pleasant after the heavy heat of moments ago which had clung to the nape of my neck as I walked. Everything inside seemed to shine - the wooden banister, the beetle-black telephone by the front door and the coloured glass in the door too was chapel-proud and sober: Cadi stood amidst the gleam of it all and the oblong mirror on the wall opposite was like the surface of a milky lake in the half-light, registering our awkwardness as two separate shadows.

"You're late tonight," she said. There wasn't the slightest rebuke in her voice, no finding fault, only an alien hoarseness binding her words to her eyes.

"Gwyneth," I said. Her name was meant to explain everything.

"It's a shame."

I tried to smile awkwardly and said: "Gwyneth's more capable than anyone realises." I didn't feel any better, though, for having said it. I wanted to grab hold of Cadi, run my fingers through her hair like last time, like every other time. Why, then, was this time different? It was as if an invisible curtain had fallen between us - we could each see the other's longing but we weren't able to reach out and touch it.

"What is it, Cadi?"

She began to push strands of her hair behind her ears as she always did when bouts of uncertainty came over her - I noticed the simplicity of the gold earrings she wore and remembered the feel of their tiny rounded coldness so often against my lips . . . . The urge to embrace her was like a physical pain because I knew at that moment that I mustn't. I followed her through into the kitchen that held all the warm untidiness of her life. This was her little domain, with its window-sill full of plants where the sun came. She had collected all kinds of paraphernalia on to a small square pinboard - amongst all this were some postcards, small exclamations of colour, the same ones there for weeks on end as if she were reluctant to take any one of them down. I thought of her as an exotic bird in a cage - the minister's wife in tight-fitting Levis gathering her dreams and securing them with drawing-pins lest they should leave her all alone.

"Eifion knows." It was as if her throat were capturing a sigh as she caught her breath on that last word.

"What? About us?" A hell of a daft question, that was. What else mattered to us other than that? The normality of the kitchen was so treacherously calm, and the table was hidden under a puff of white lace and some corduroy and shiny bits of something else that I didn't know the name of. Remnants of exotic-looking, expensive material piled in a heap and a sewing-basket lying open amidst the gaiety of it all. How could she think of getting started on her sewing, knowing she had this to tell me?

She followed my eyes and smiled a lopsided smile.

"Costumes for the children's pageant."

And there she was, looking into my soul, her eyes the same colour as her faded jeans - a pale washed-ever-so-many-times kind of blue.

"Christ, Cadi! Tell me, how can you be such a - minister's wife?"

"I've no choice, have I, Dafydd?"

But it was as she was saying this that she came to me and the awkwardness was pushed aside. Her fingertips were gentle, familiar as they read between the lines of tension which had taken over every sinew in my body. We knew that this would be the last time; it was all almost sacred, ritualistic and clean and final, like washing a corpse.

It was easier then, somehow. Easier to face things. Because there was no turning back. It was as if I'd been forced into having some kind of painful but necessary amputation and I could still feel the tingling of my absent limb. I left the house in the early hours and the night enclosed me in a cloying embrace as if I were thrusting my shoulder into a spider's web. By now even the breeze had spent itself and lay weary. The damp was sweet, freshening the evening right through, and each tree was gathering the raindrops into the nape of its neck like a girl taking a shower. Jesus, it was all so clear - every leaf, every star, every swollen black vein between each cloud coming into focus for the first time as though I were looking through new lenses that were so clean they were stinging my eyes . . . .

* * * * * * * * * * * * * * * * *

"Deio?"

I was ashamed of myself for letting my mind wander across her secret, and I kept the sudden flush of that shame deep inside me until it began gnawing coldly at my spine. Her smile was still a child's smile, its radiance awakening her eyes. She was nearly thirty years old and she could still look in wonder at the little every-day things that I never bothered to remember existed; she could still get carried away without being embarrassed by it. Had I been offered a king's ransom at that moment to define my feelings I could not have responded, could not have made any sense of any of it. It's easier today, easier to touch a memory and turn it over in my hands, then to hold it upside down in the cold light of day to look for its hallmark. And its easier to admit, albeit to myself, that my insecurity that day stemmed from my own envy of her.

"You're not cross with me, are you, Deio?" There was a kind of childish imploring still entwined in her words, that old, old hankering for assurance and approval. That all-too-sincere, all-too-modest whiter than whiteness which made her so dependent on us all. And yet . . . . "He's kind. Kind and gentle with me . . . . "

For once I was amazed that she had not waited for me to answer her question. And for once I did not hasten to do so in case I punctuated the flow of her words, I suppose, words that were an almost unearthly combination of a sensible, sensual young woman and an innocent little girl infatuated with something she knew nothing about whatsoever.

"We hold each other ever so tightly." She clasped her own arms about herself, as if she were wearing her happiness next to her skin. "And he kisses my hair . . . . "

"You don't have to tell me, Gwyneth."

She shared her secret so openly - those sacred, hidden things that you cannot know about, cannot understand unless you've been loved yourself. I thought of Cadi; wondered if she too still imprisoned the years and the butterfly kisses between her hands. Gwyneth had read me again, it seemed, picked crumbs from my daydream:

"You understand, don't you, Deio?" There was still a kind of mystical bond between us, something superior to mental age and the passing of time, something rare that I wasn't going to cheapen by patronising her.

"Look, I'm sorry, Gwyn. For leaving you that time. The night of the storm."

She held her head to one side, like a confused kitten. I understood how a man could fall in love with her.

"When you went to Cadi?"

"Yes."

"Doesn't matter now. That was a long time ago."

"It still pricks my conscience. When I get to thinking about it."

"You said I was a big girl. Capable enough. 'Dad'll be home tomorrow.' That's what you said before you went. And there was thunder far away in the sky."

Coming from anyone else those words would have been deliberately coated with an angry disappointment fed by years of waiting for a chance to get even. But Gwyneth didn't know how to bear a grudge. "I knew everything would be alright when tomorrow came, see. And it was night-time, anyway. Not long to go till morning. And I slept tight and forgot to listen for you turning the key in the lock. And Pwtan warmed my feet . . . . "

So I wasn't the only one to remember the details of that night. But in their innocence her memories were full of the best things - of gentle slumber and the warmth of a cat until tomorrow touched her in shavings of light and filled her room like a shower of sawdust. Unknowingly, she offered me her forgiveness when she looked at me through her secret and said:

"And now I've got a lover that no one must know about."

She wanted to tell me. She held his name in the corner of her mouth like a hot peppermint . . . . No, Gwyneth, don't tell . . . . She didn't understand that sharing a secret was like unwrapping a gift - a short-lived, impulsive pleasure before the magic was lost. The child in her eyes was all excitement but the transparent lines of her cheekbones and dewy lips belonged to a young woman in love. That's why I turned away, changed the subject - changed the direction of things, maybe too soon, so that she looked at me without understanding and her face was bruised in shadow as if all the light in the room had at that very moment retreated behind her. I didn't want her to be caught out by her own innocence, but she didn't understand; all she saw was my indifference and she turned away from me, her shoulders as if they were collapsing beneath the weight of her clothes . . . . No, Deio Bach, Gwyneth won't tell . . . .

It only took about three days then for the secret to betray itself. I went into the house as usual - not being especially quiet or unusually noisy. It was a usual sort of a day. To be honest, everything had been oddly ordinary following the unreality of the day before. It's obvious that Gwyneth didn't hear me. Neither did he. She was wearing green and the back kitchen was embroidered in light where the shadows of the leaves on the trees outside cast their lacy patterns across the walls. Green has always suited her. The colour of her very first grown-up dress. 'Look how pretty I am, Deio! Look how pretty!' - and she twirled and twirled - like a flower-fairy wrapped up in a leaf - 'Pretty! Pretty! Look, I'm pretty . . . . ' The colour of the garden itself. And we all stood at the edge of her pirouette and watched her sacrifice her little white wrists to a fickle sun.

That's how I found myself that afternoon too. Standing at the edge of a rare kind of exultation and being afraid to breathe lest it should disappear. And Gwyneth's eyes were still saying 'Look how pretty I am today!' But she was looking at him and the stillness was so still it was as if the image wasn't in front of me at all, only inside my head like the bare bones of an old dream.

It wasn't the fact that I knew him that floored me. Or even the fact that he was a married man. It wasn't those things which made my breath cloud up inside me; it was the otherworldliness of this picture of the two of them that made me feel as if I'd caught them in each other's arms. Because it felt like that through the sepia silence. Their fingertips touched lightly across the table and the room was a capsule of light before the afternoon would give up its last sigh. It was the very same light, the same light that Gwyneth saw the morning after the storm, a white veil to be worn by a flawless tomorrow. Pure. Purer. Purest. Gwyneth. Fair-skinned Gwyneth. Lily-white hands. A smile like the shadow of a flower.

I went out softly, leaving them in the light.

A Half-Sinner

It was a breathtaking adjudication, and the crowd was silent in the heat of the pavilion. I heard words like 'compelling' and 'anguish'. When lines were quoted from the winning sequence of poems, the silence drew breath. And his nom-de-plume sang inside my head as if it were bruising itself against the walls of an empty room . . . .

* * * * * * * * * * * * * * * * *

He was the brightest student in his year. He came to me one afternoon with his essay tucked neatly inside a plastic wallet.

"It's raining," he said diffidently, as if he felt he had to apologise for being careful of his work.

"You've completed it well before time, Dafydd."

His lips tightened modestly. It was as if he were afraid of being praised. I noticed him waiting, unsure; he stood with his shoulder to the door-frame, his height making him awkward. He waited for me to ask him. I was the tutor after all. And he depended on that.

"Things going all right, then?"

He shrugged his shoulders as if a chill went through him.

"I'm enjoying the course," he said politely. Too quietly. That wasn't the answer he had wanted to give. I was aware of the naked bar of the electric fire like a red, pointless scream in a room that was too big.

"Why don't you sit down for a minute? We haven't had much time for a chat recently . . . . "

He stepped forward so that the door might shut behind him and the draught stopped suddenly. His eyes embraced everything without actually looking at anything. He stretched out his long legs as he tried to sit comfortably; I felt sorry I couldn't offer him a better chair. I was glad that the untidiness of the desk drew his eyes momentarily away from me. He suddenly noticed the small volume I had been reading some moments before.

"Yeats," he said, as if he had just spotted a friend. There was enthusiasm in his voice now.

"Hard to beat the Irish for a dose of passion," I answered, and realised, even as I spoke, that I sounded rather glib. But I don't think he was listening then.

"I can identify with Yeats." He raised his eyes suddenly; it was obvious that he hadn't intended to sound smug. "That is, I believe I understand how he felt . . . . "

Dozens of fresh-faced young men had sat here before him and poured out their feelings to me after some poet or other had awakened their consciences. Ideals were healthy things to have, at his age, as long as they didn't get out of hand. I began to have doubts. There was something, some kind of upset . . . . So I began to fish around a bit.

"Yeats's patriotism can touch people . . . . "

He ventured to look into my eyes.

"Not only his patriotism. There are other things - the other thing . . . . " He paused. "It's a shame she didn't have a nicer name."

"Who?"

"Maude Gonne."

I stifled a sigh. Who was she, then, I wondered? This long-haired little flirt who'd broken his heart and then spurned him. A college scarf and a mini skirt made for a heady combination when there were stars over Siliwen.

"It happens to us all, you know, Dafydd."

He looked intently at my shirt-collar where the material had begun to fray, evidently finding that difficult to believe.

"I'm not trying to make light of your feelings. It's a hell of a blow - the break-up of a relationship . . . . " I sounded too fatherly while his own eyes bored through the cliches. I tried to give him a chance. To be professionally tactful, leaving pauses in the right places. But he refused to fill the empty spaces between the sentences. I persevered:

"This is an important time for you, Dafydd. You must try and fight it - not let the work suffer . . . . " Even though that hadn't happened as yet. The standard of his work was consistent, mature. He had this rare kind of perception which was difficult to define. Yes, this fellow mattered.

"I know it's difficult - having to see her on campus every day . . . . "

For a moment I imagined him to be looking at me rather pityingly. He took his hands from his pockets and knitted his fingers together.

"She was our minister's wife," he said evenly. "Back home, in Foel."

He didn't say it for the effect it would have. It was obvious that my silence unsettled him. I stared at him for some moments until he said:

"I thought I'd write . . . . "

"Rather than suffocate."

The edge of his lip curled. It wasn't a smile.

"Something like that." His hands were restless. "The catharsis, I suppose. Isn't it pain that inspires every writer?"

I understood why Yeats had appealed. The remains of the damp from outside had formed a tailed web across the shoulders of his jacket. He took an untidy roll of paper from his inside pocket. The attempts of the would-be poet. We both knew that it was my turn to say something. I did the cowardly thing. Stole the words of a greater man:

" 'I sometimes hold it half a sin . . . . '"

" ' . . . . to put in words the grief I feel.' " He finished the quotation for me and his hands grew still. I should have realised.

"Of course. You would be familiar with Tennyson."

He smiled a tight little smile.

"I read as much as I can."

"And now the muse is beckoning you too?"

He noticed that my eyes were being drawn towards the

pages in his hand.

"Maybe you could have a look at one or two of them . . .?"

I might have been flattered by the fact that he had so much respect for my literary judgement had he not drawn low that veil of uncertainty over his eyes. He didn't want me to be kind to him. I felt his face upon me as I read.

"They're not lies," he said defensively. And maybe that was the trouble with them. Here was his own soul, offering its secret like an open hand.

"This is the raw material, isn't it, Dafydd?"

He didn't answer. We both knew that this was his confession before he could move on. He reached carefully for his paper. He wanted to make it easy for me. The sound of the paper tearing was as clinical and measured as if he were breaking a loaf of bread between his hands; and they were so white too, like bread also.

"Too many words," he said. There was something akin to relief in his voice.

"Too much grief, perhaps?"

He relaxed the muscles of his face a little then: "But that's only half a sin, isn't it? Don't you agree?"

He was referring to the words of the poet we'd been quoting earlier on.

"So that's how you see yourself then, is it, Dafydd? Some kind of half-sinner?"

He was able to smile now; his poems were in pieces on the desk and it didn't matter at all. He had a poet's eyes, and for now that was enough. When he got up to go he was older and his coat had dried.

"From the pain to the pen then," he said. He laughed shyly to lighten his words, a sudden cough of a sound clicking softly in his throat like the lifting of a latch.

His words hovered silently between the four walls long after he'd gone. When I returned to the poetry of Yeats it seemed as if he had embraced his pain with Dafydd Parry's eyes.

* * * * * * * * * * * * * * * * *

He sang about dreams, fragile as mountain mist, and of the cold kisses of the hoar-frost along his shoes. He salvaged his hours from the flow and they stood still for him beneath the light with dew upon their breasts. He sang about tomorrow with yesterday warm upon the nape of his neck, like a girl's breath . . . .

It was an intricate chair, high-backed, frozen within a saucer of light as the 'Half-Sinner' was escorted to the stage. He sat in it with his back straight, his height giving him an unusual dignity. And he closed his fingers tightly about the arms of this chair, about the complicated beauty of the carvings, as if he were pressing his secret into the yellow wood. His eyes embraced everyone and everything, but you could have sworn in all truth that he wasn't really looking at anyone or anything. Because those were the kind of eyes he had; eyes that could turn yesterday into tomorrow. A poet's eyes.

The Girl who saw the Colours of the Rain

She was about thirty, tall and slender. That's what made her appear younger than her age, I suppose. It was her supple slenderness that reminded me of a sapling. That and her eyes. They were blue and green, green or blue, blue and blue-green alternately . . . . . And alternately they filled up with wonder and fear - no, perhaps not fear - it was a kind of quick nervousness, like in the eyes of a wild but harmless animal standing on the edge of a strange place. I couldn't help but stare at her. And she in turn stared at the rain drumming desperately onto the roof of the long veranda.

It would have been usual for me to begin chatting straightaway to someone forced to shelter with me like this - especially with there being only the two of us. But she took no notice of me. It wasn't that she ignored me intentionally. It was as if she hadn't realised that I was there at all. A shadow of a smile lay across the line of her lips. She stood like a living statue, all senses, listening, watching, breathing some faraway secret hidden amongst the needles of rain - a rain lending its own colour-of-nothing to everything; it was as if someone was trying to etch out the daylight with a fine-pointed pencil. The rain lulled my senses too. It beat down softly upon the earth as the leaves on the trees dripped like tongues. I was caught between the rhythms of the wet and felt guilty, somehow, for taking advantage of the fact that there was no-one else there to see me staring at her. To see me comb through the veil of her hair with the corner of my eye. It was incredible hair, falling so closely along the line of her shoulders that it seemed her whole body had been carved from a single piece of smooth wood. I imagined touching that hair and feeling warmth beneath its cool sheen. When a watery flash of lightning broke through the greyness I saw her step back and then forward again just as quickly towards the rail of the veranda like a child whose curiosity gets the better of its nervousness. I noticed the sudden patches of damp mottling the front of her shoes and stifled an inexplicable urge to grasp her hand and pull her back into the shelter. The restaurant-sounds coming from behind us were welcoming and civilized. I could easily have imagined myself leading her inside and watching those water-colour eyes melt over the heat from her coffee-cup. Whilst I tried to laugh inwardly at my own weakness and yearned at the same time for her to notice my existence, she looked at me. Suddenly, spontaneously, as wide-eyed as the matchbox-lightning spitting white into the void of the afternoon. And she said:

"A storm. I like watching storms."

Her eyes danced off me then, just as suddenly. I didn't know how to hold her attention. The next thing I said to her just had to be interesting, amusing even. But all I could think of saying was:

"Watch out, or you'll get wet out there!"

I was fifty, been married for ever, and sadly out of practice. But she didn't appear to have heard me.

"It's easing off now," she said. "The rain's stopping." But she didn't look in my direction when she said that. In fact, she probably wasn't really talking to me at all. I became, for the first time, painfully conscious of my expanding waistline. I couldn't hold a conversation. My mind was lame, the words I might have said limping with their tails behind them between the restaurant noises behind us and the intermittent pattering of the rain trailing off into damp tendrils along the outside path.

"I'm not afraid. Are you?" Again, her comments were unexpected, reaching me from nowhere.

"What . . . . ?"

"Thunder and lightning. I'm not afraid of it at all. A childish thing to say; she sounded almost shy. Was she teasing me? Flirting, even? It was difficult to say. There was something different about the pale, slim girl with hair the colour of treacle. She didn't have the poise, the graceful reserve I would have expected to see in someone of her age and beauty. Then again, something about this way of hers held a certain allure. She swayed lightly back and forth and kept her balance by holding on to the wooden rail. Now and again she threw back her head and lifted her chin to the dampness that was spitting in our direction. While I cursed the inconvenience of the rain and became greedily aware of the fresh coffee and cake smells wafting through the half-open door, she was totally oblivious to everything apart from what she could see in the gardens in front of her. Not that she was staring at the flowers - it was as if she was looking into them, between them, seeing colour in the sheet of grey dampness covering everywhere like a heavy veil.

"I'm waiting for my brother."

Her sentences were sudden and unprompted, wanting nothing in return. She spoke like someone used to not being given answers, and who was painfully comfortable listening to her own conversation.

"You're here on a day trip, then?"

"No. I'm with my brother." She wasn't trying to be clever. She added: "He won't be long, you'll see."

I didn't bother to explain: Well, I'm here on the Chapel outing. Have to go every year - one of the deacons, you see. A pillar of the bloody community, selling raffles for the Blaid and Glenys the wife buying my underpants in Marks in packs of three. Until now, today's been bloody boring but Bodhyfryd Gardens are one of Glenys's favourite places - and I've given her the slip an hour and a half ago and when she gets hold of me there'll be hell to pay for wandering off and leaving her . . . . No. I didn't bother explaining. It wasn't important, wasn't unprompted, sudden and shy. With someone else I'd have told a funny story about escaping the wife's clutches. But not with this girl. Instinctively, somehow, I knew that witty anecdotes of that variety would be lost on her. The strange, unknown, amazing girl in whom I didn't know why I had taken such an interest in so short a time. Towards whom I didn't know how to explain this gentle attraction I felt.

The rain stopped and left an emptiness in its wake. People appeared hesitantly, one by one, from different directions and picked their way like delicate cats into the no-man's land of dampness. Within minutes a comparatively young man strode across the path in front of us towards our sheltering-place. I guessed him to be around forty. The same tall stance, the same slim build, the same pale skin but the dark hair had begun to show signs of grey. This was the brother. The look on his face was an odd combination of concern and boredom. He walked towards her without once lifting his eyes as if an invisible cord was drawing him towards her. She looked at him expectantly, her face all aglow. I stared at them blatantly as if I were watching a scene in a film.

"You alright?" asked the brother.

"Yes. Alright," she replied, like an echo. The rhythm of their conversation was like the rhythm of the rain earlier on, their words bouncing off each other and falling in droplets. Then they noticed me, both of them, at the same time, at one glance. He was the one to venture with:

"Appalling weather we're having."

"Yes. Appalling." What was it about this man that made people want to echo his words? His eyes, maybe. They were bottomless, taking possession of our words.

"It's nothing like summer."

"Nothing like," I agreed, and smiled inwardly because I was doing it again, awkwardly following his words as if I were reading Braille. Bringing myself closer to his conversation.

"I know your face," he said. His sentences too were unexpected, uninvited, their suddenness rolling off me. I didn't offer him my name, just stared back at him lamely, challenging him,

I suppose, to prove himself. He did.

"You used to come over and give me piano lessons!"

And instinctively I looked at his hands, at his long fingers which were slim and pale like the rest of him. I remembered those hands then, remembered their talent. And remembered him - a drawn, sensitive fourteen-year-old, throwing his grief into the music whilst the earth was too fresh upon his mother's grave for them to put a headstone there. "We haven't been able to put the stone there yet . . . . " The father speaking without looking at anyone, making conversation because it was the civilized thing to do. They were the words of a lost man apologising for something over which he had no control, and that thin, dark-haired little girl clinging tightly to his hand. The boy sat in front of the heavy piano and caressed it with his eyes. When his fingers brushed against the melody it was as if blood were flowing warm from a cut. I heard myself whisper 'adaggio' and his hands slowed their pace like ailing moths. It was summer. I walked home with the grief of the three of them singing in my ears. The heat formed droplets beneath my shirt and honeysuckle was sickly-sweet in the hedgerows. My feet moved to the slow rhythms of the music in my head. It was hot, so hot, and the afternoon swam. Great yellow heat, taking no heed, and the children of Cae Aur without a mother.

I realised I'd been too long chasing my thoughts. But he still stared patiently at me, confident I'd remember.

"It's been years," I said and the tenderness in my own voice surprised me.

"Do you still teach the piano?"

I shook my head. We were being drawn already into the trivial small talk which thrives among strangers. We mentioned the weather, and tried to make our voices sound interesting. I ventured to ask how their father was. In an old people's home by now, he said. She lowered her eyes at this and looked sad. I regretted having asked at all. She held on to her brother's hand and in my mind's eye I pictured her long ago in her father's hand; the cold piano and the hot sun and the earth not settled enough for them to put a stone on the grave . . . .

So we chatted like that, the two of us, while the day's temperature continued to rise and the rain became nothing more than mottled stains on the surface of things. His sister was quiet, her eyes wandering slowly off our faces and returning shy and restless like birds landing. He'd brought her here on an outing, he said. Being as the weather was so nice when they set off that morning. A day out like this did her good sometimes. It wasn't often she had the chance to get out. He said all this as if she wasn't there, wasn't a part of the picture of the three of us. It was obvious that he cared for her but his affection was too tight around her, his words closing in on her, floating above her head. I thought of a tame rabbit shut in for its own protection as I looked at her. A pretty, silky-black rabbit. And I imagined setting it free.

"Ifor!" Glenys's voice from somewhere too close before the flowery gaudiness of her frock boiled over into view. "Where've you been? What came over you, wandering off and leaving me . . . " And the children of Cae Aur who weren't children any more disappeared, leaving their portraits sketched into my mind like the tendrils of a dream.

"Glenys love, you wouldn't believe who I've just been talking to . . . . "

"I've been looking for you everywhere like a fool! Refused lunch with Lydia and Mrs Jones the Minister in case you'd be waiting for me . . . . "

"Sorry."

"Yes, I should think so, too. I haven't eaten since that ten o'clock cup of tea. My stomach thinks my throat's been cut . . . . !"

"Look, Glen, we'll go in here - there's a place for a cuppa..."

Something, anything, to shut up that bloody tirade which was bulldozing through all that loveliness inside my head.

"Come on in, then," she said sulkily but more softly. It was as if I were stepping straight out of one world and into another, speaking and smiling with somebody else's lips.

"What'll you have, Ifor? You're not listening at all... "

But her words stayed outside me like a draught outside a door. I noticed the fine lines at the corners of her lips, dragging, dragging downwards. I fell in love with her in yesterday's simplicity when I was someone else and she was young. Now yesterday was lost in the mist and I was staring through the new sun that was being pressed, white, into the table, seeing green and blue and the little shards of rain and washing my eyes in the shine of those sudden moments when the pale, slim girl looked at me and said that she wasn't afraid . . . .

"Two coffees?"

Two words. Two cups in two saucers and two souls circling each other to the sound of other people's voices. I could do nothing apart from listen to the discourse of the voices in my head, recreating what had just been to the sad accompaniment of an old tune. Had I been a character in a story I would have chosen that moment to walk out; to follow the girl through the crowd leaving Glenys to stare after me, open-mouthed. I burnt my mouth by gulping the hot coffee and felt oddly peeved because of the pain. I had been mooching about for ages on the edge of a dream and now I couldn't allow myself to enter it - nothing's supposed to hurt in a dream. If I were in a story, well, that would have been another thing, but this wasn't a story either. I was me, in a cafe with my wife drinking a too-hot cup of coffee. Every movement, every stance, the words, the sounds - all I heard and saw - hung in a void and I was trying to keep myself apart from it by spinning a protective web around my feelings. A group of people walked past our table. The women left wafts of their perfume behind them as they passed; the youngest of them wore a light-coloured summer dress down to her ankles - the same kind of dress . . . . the hair long . . . . but she wasn't as tall, as slender, as transparently beautiful . . . .

"We still live at Cae Aur, you know. Don't you go that way sometimes . . . . ? You must drop in some time . . . . "

That's what he said. Before the afternoon swallowed them. Cae Aur . . . . still live at Cae Aur . . . . do you go that way . . . . do you? . . . . why not drop in . . . . ? His words invited me, like tomorrow and the day after and the days after that, sprouting up white in her footsteps too. Leaving a pathway from one dream to another. She looked shyly at me over her shoulder. He turned too and saw her dawdle, and leave an uncertain smile behind her, like a child thinking twice about going home. He reached his hand out to her.

"Come on, now, Gwyneth."

And I remembered. The heat of an old sun splitting and the opiate honeysuckle in the hedgerow. The girl with the words overflowing from her eyes like daylight through a lace cloth. The girl who saw the colours of the rain, with a name to suit her smile.

A Pleasant Room

It's a pleasant room. Spacious and white and warm. Catches all the sun early in the morning, sun that fondles the chairs, feeling the emptiness where their thoughts have been.

They don't like the sun. Some of them crease their faces at it tetchily until their eyes disappear. It makes fun of them, and they know that perfectly well, pretending not to watch it as it tightens the noose upon their lost youth and suspends it, yellow, along the walls.

There's a feel of hoar-frost. If they'd allowed Garmon Parry to go out into the morning he'd have felt it damp across the nape of his neck. But even through glass the exquisite melancholy with the smell of summer on its fingers reminds him how to weep. The early morning cold is worse, they say, when a man has grown old. So he sits in the artificial heat with both his hands on his knees. He's straight-backed for his age, his face unyielding like the face of a rock.

New clouds are thrusting into the picture that fills the window-frame. He doesn't know why the sky has to move constantly. Changing places. Changing colour. The untidiness of the cloud disturbs him, as if a cushion has ripped in his mind. How can he gather the fragments back together again? They're as fragile as thoughts, insistent upon slipping through his fingers without leaving even a trace. They're clever. Crafty. Like live things. Expanding . . . . fragmenting . . . . yet always there . . . .

"They'll be here soon, you'll see."

This one's wearing a blue uniform like the others and she knows his name's Garmon. It's as if she knows him, knows this place. As if she's well used to it all.

But he never saw her before in his life, even though she looks like someone far away inside his head. That was the kind of place this was, full of different people who looked exactly alike. Everyone with similar-sized smiles. Hands clearing away, voices carrying . . . .

"Come now, Garmon. Slippers on . . . . "

"Well done! A clean plate today . . . . "

"Now then, Garmon Parry, a tiny tiny spoonful . . . . just to please me . . . .?"

Voices of an echo. That's my boy . . . . your mother's son . . . . a spoonful of medicine and a spoonful of jam . . . . Yesterday's as clear as opening a book where the print is bold. He sees his mother's hands soft between the lines and he likes to warm his mind on the sweet smell of airing sheets. There was someone else. He remembers the perfume of her hair soft against his cheek. This isn't his mother. She's there, in his head, a fragile vision, reaching out her arms . . . .

"They'll be here soon."

He doesn't give any sign of having understood and neither does the nurse expect a response. The busy blueness of her clothes is cold against his eyes. Her chat is so motherly. Always the same. Coaxing. Persuading. The simplicity of her vocabulary lulling him. He knows that there are longer words than hers. They're so close sometimes that he can feel their eyes glinting at him. He fishes for them in the pool of his brain where the water's black - sudden, starry sounds with little knives of tails restless in his mind, challenging, probing, provoking. Damn them. They're taking advantage now. Plaguing him and he's so tired . . . .

"There we are, Garmon - won't you have this rug over your lap? It's a chilly old morning out there - there you are - well, really, you're behaving well for me today . . . . . "

"Can't . . . . just can't . . . . "

"What was that?"

"Can't catch them."

"Can't catch who, then, Garmon dear?"

"Well, these darned fish!" he says and lifts his eyes.

"Of course." She's used to it, smoothing her words over him.

"They're slipping through my hands - all tails . . . . " And the straight-backed old gentleman feels the memories clouding his vision.

"Your eyes are watering a bit this morning - I said it was colder, didn't I? Wait a minute . . . . "

The little paper tissue is painfully light against his cheekbones . . . .

"Come on, now . . . . you don't need to fret, for goodness' sake! I was only wiping your eyes so that you'd feel more comfortable . . . ."

He despises her tender interference. They're his tears.

* * * * * * * * * * * * * * * * *

"You're very quiet."

She's motionless too, and has clasped her arms tightly around herself. She looks shivery.

"I'm cold."

He turns the car heater up. The hot air conditioning tickles the ends of her hair and makes her want to smile. Within a short time she's loosened her arms and is resting her head against the back of the seat. These are the very best mornings, shiny fresh ones and the paint on them not yet dry. Her senses stretch out to the low purr of the engine, arching their backs, purring along with it in the warmth.

"I'm hot now!"

"Bloody hell, Gwyneth!" And he leans forward again, deleting the instant hot air in one movement. But she enjoyed that, the breath that was so tantalizingly close, so shamelessly bold, like a great, gentle animal venturing near to her.

"Why did you switch that off?"

"You said it was too hot . . . . "

"No, I didn't!"

"Well, yes, you did. You just said so!"

"Didn't say I was too hot . . . . "

"What . . . .!"

"Just hot. Nice and hot. I wasn't too hot . . . . "

"Christ Almighty . . . . "

"Don't swear. You shouldn't swear . . . . "

"I'm not . . . . "

"Yes you are. You're swearing. And you're a liar." She isn't afraid of him and he knows it. He'll never really lose his temper. Even when they were children it was as if he'd learnt to lose his temper carefully rather than hurt her. Nothing's changed. Only that he's older. She still has her childhood lying hidden inside her head like a tiny sparkling precious stone.

"Swearing. Lying. And cross." She plagues him. "You're cross too."

He lets her words fall into the engine's hum.

"You're always cross when we go to see Dad."

He doesn't respond. She's just skinned his senses with her simple words: not long now, not much further to go. But he can smell the place already - too much old age under one roof and the walls too white, too square. Each time he goes in through those new doors he's forced to admit his failure. How many times did he have to try and justify the whole thing to himself? He remembers again the encouraging words of doctors and social workers that did nothing to ease his conscience:

"You're doing the right thing, Mr Parry . . . . "

"Your father will get the specialist care that he needs . . . . "

So they took him to wash him and feed him with a spoon because his mind had pieces missing like an old jig-saw puzzle. And because he doesn't remember how to remember, they praise him for opening his mouth wide and swallowing his food tidily; they wring out his frustration from the face-cloth and throw it away with the water.

They hinted at that time that Gwyneth should go into care too. That she should go away for a little while, now and then. So that he could have a break. Wasn't the added responsibility of looking after his sister going to take its toll on him too in the long run? Dafydd flatly refused. Never ever. He would never even consider it. They stopped hinting. They were only doing their jobs. He remembers all their reasoning each time he comes within sight of the white building where they try and stifle the hospital smells with the smell of polish and bowls of pot-pourri; but there are too many flowers in too many vases dying without anyone noticing and too many mute strangers in armchairs to fool anyone into thinking that this is a proper home. Dafydd comforts himself in the knowledge that his father hasn't a clue where he is anyway. But Gwyneth would know if she were being sent away. She'd know where she was but she wouldn't know why. No, he wouldn't do that to Gwyneth. She wasn't the one who'd changed. She was the same as always, always would be. Not like his father, distancing himself by the hour, his eyes emptying slowly like buckets with holes in them. He's never thought of Gwyneth as a burden. She's his kid sister. Will always be so. Hers is the most natural company in the world. She's there constantly, holding his life steady.

He remembers as if it were yesterday when they took him to the home. Gwyneth sitting with her father in the back of the car and he was holding tightly onto her hand because he couldn't remember her name. He remembers coming home, two of them instead of three, and the combination of guilt and grief knotting together in his head. And he remembers the day after, clean, full of washing-smells and soap suds, and she not taking on that she'd been crying. A drying day . . . .

* * * * * * * * * * * * * * * * *

He was holding the washing-basket for her - and she was busy, practical, keeping her father about her by filling the line with his clothes.

"When will we be fetching Dad home, Deio?" Because he'd always come home from everywhere. "Maybe he'll be back before I get a chance to take him his clean pyjamas!"

"Shouldn't think so, love. He needs time to get better."

"He will get better, then?"

The sudden doubt in her voice gave her a deceptive kind of maturity; it was as if she couldn't hold on to it long enough. Her mind toyed with all her fears without knowing how to touch them, like a flame in a draught.

"Of course he will." His answer coming too late to be a part of her question. And she, without noticing it, pressing on:

"He'll come home when they've written back the names of things in his head."

The sky itself looked like a cloth hung out to dry. A flutter of starlings passed dirtily across it, their bits of wings like snatches of joined-up writing. In their inky-coloured distance Dafydd could see chunks of his own confession where the day had caught hold of them and challenged him to read them.

Gwyneth gradually got used to her father not being in the house. Dafydd wondered whether she'd half-realised that he wouldn't come home to live with them again. He watched her working silently through her feelings. In her child-mind, her father had left her and she was angry with him. She refused to talk when they went to see him. She became sulky and sad. That was a phase, and it passed. She adapted as a child would have done, and her sweetness returned. Her child-like hope spurred her on yet again and the future was a faraway, uncertain thing, floating magically between now and forever. And one day, some tomorrow or other in the midst of it all, when the sun was full and round like a child's cheeks, her father would return.

* * * * * * * * * * * * * * * * *

"Sorry, Gwyn." She looks at him. He looks at the road. Feels her eyes on him. Steers the car between the white gates. "Sorry for being tetchy. Being cross. And I didn't mean to swear at you . . . . "

"Fuck off!"

"What did you say?"

"That's swearing, isn't it? Proper swearing. You didn't use a nasty swear-word like that, did you, Dei? So it's alright. I'll forgive you this once!" She knows he's dumbstruck and she smiles without moving her lips, enjoying the effect of her mischievousness.

"You're a little terror, Gwyneth!"

In those few seconds, Dafydd sees someone as old as her age, and inside he weeps for what she might have been.

* * * * * * * * * * * * * * * * *

It's a white room . . . . white . . . . white . . . . so snow white, yes, so fair, so slender . . . . a white cat of a cloud curls up tightly on the edge of his mind . . . . the edge of his bed . . . . white sheet, white nightgown and her hair still and smooth down her back like a lake under moonlight . . . . white, white, white - yes, slender-white . . . .

They're used to the distant look, the not-recognising. But today he stares in wonder at Gwyneth. Her long white dress has awakened something in his eyes, and he reaches out his hand and calls her by her mother's name.

"Bet, what took you so long?"

"No, Dad. It's me." And Dafydd turns his back on it all, holding his jaw tense. "It's Gwyneth, Dad."

Dafydd doesn't want to look at his father. He despises the empty pools of his eyes now without being ashamed because the disappointment has stayed too long in Gwyneth's face; it's as if her sadness has been captured there for ever, but it's a novice painter's canvas and the eyes are too still. This bloody place depresses him - this room that's too white where the sun jaundices the walls. He doesn't want to look at any of the other faces either, faces hovering dully above their earth-coloured jumpers and rugs. Brown and grey and soul-less green; he thinks of cemeteries and lichen on stone surfaces. There's one old dear in a too-pink cardigan who insists upon thrusting her image into the corner of his eye, violating the mossy monotony of everything like an old sweet-wrapper floating on a stagnant duckpond. He sees his responsibility close thinly upon him in grey strands and his simple, sweet sister kneeling in front of the father who does not recognise her. He's going to steal these moments for his own self-pity until Garmon Parry's voice halts the flow of his mind like a sudden exclamation mark . . . .

"Gwyneth?" Her name is a question, an accident of a word that's just fallen from between his lips.

"Gwyneth . . . . yes, must be . . . ."

The sound of the word tickles the edges of his senses - a hair ribbon in a breeze . . . . red . . . . a little red dress . . . . a frill . . . . the smell of the sea and ice-cream, the tail of a kite clacking softly. . . . Something stands between him and the remembering of it. He stares again into the fragments of a sky that is still provoking him.

Gwyneth looks up, startled, as if looking for his voice with her eyes. She tries to read his reveries like she used to a long time ago and follows his glances way up high. There are clouds in his eyes too. And suddenly, like he used to, he turns to her and releases his mind to her. It's alright for her to ask now:

"What is it? What's up there? What d'you see in the sky today, Dad?"

"All kinds of things," he says. "Dragons' mouths smoking all over the sky!"

The little girl within her becomes a flush of sudden

excitement.

"Are they talking, Dad? Are they? What are they saying...?"

"Who?"

"Those dragons!"

It's like there's no window, like there's no cold pane of glass between them and the world. He's holding her hand now. He hasn't held her hand in a long time. Or talked to her either. But it doesn't matter. She's long forgotten that already, and remembers the good things, remembers when he drew stories for her from beneath the skin of everything and the tweed of his jacket rough against her cheek.

"D'you see that big old dragon there - that one . . . . over here . . . ."

"With its cheeks ready to blow!"

"Yes, that's the one. It's the chief dragon, keeps all the others in order . . . . "

"Those little ones . . . . "

"Because they play around too much, slashing their tails, blowing secrets into each other's ears."

Dafydd stares. He can only see a cloudy sky. He stands there on the edge of their fairytale world with his hands in his pockets. Through the window in front of him the tarmac drive stretches neatly to the gates, its surface dotted with the occasional fallen leaf, withered too soon. He can't see the gates from here.

"We'll have to set off home quite soon now."

That worries him. The journey home. He imagines how Gwyneth's chatter will be, full of her father and her hopes fluttering in front of her. Her eyes turn to him but for once he can't read them.

"He'll be getting tired, you know, Gwyn."

She gets up slowly off her knees, smoothing her dress with her hands and looking at him awkwardly.

"He's had a good day today!" The nurse is there, hovering, ready to take charge again, and the air around Dafydd's nostrils is heavy with cooking smells.

"Gwyneth and her father have had quite a chat this time, Mr Parry!"

"Yes." It's unlikely that Garmon will remember within the hour that they've been there at all. He doesn't have to remind this fresh-faced nurse of that. His father's condition makes fun of them all. It's that kind of thing. A fickle illness that turns your mind over so that it can write its own song on the back of it.

"Come on, Gwyneth. We'll go now . . . . "

She turns around obediently to follow him. He's surprised, uncomfortable, noticing how her eyes are judging the urgency in his voice.

"Wait, Deio. I've forgotten . . . . "

Suddenly and shyly she drops a kiss on her father's cheek.

"Thanks for the story, Dad."

Garmon Parry's face is already becoming a mask, as if his senses are numbing again, slowly, one by one.

"He's getting tired, that's what it is . . . . " There's an apologetic lilt in the nurse's voice and Dafydd can feel the touch of Gwyneth's hand upon his arm.

"Are we ready to go now, Deio?"

Their father's eyes are already wandering, following the shadows which are mottling the walls. But Gwyneth doesn't look back. She has soft soles under her shoes. They squeak funnily as the two of them walk across the smooth block floor towards the front door.

"Little pigs suckling!" she says. Her loud whisper tickles his ear, making them both want to laugh. But they daren't do that. Not here. Not until the heavy door slams shut behind them.

"You and your little pigs!"

"Dad used to say that! D'you remember? When he had new shoes . . . . "

They don't laugh after all.

"He's happy here, you know." It's as if she's just decided that for herself. "He'd never have been able to tell me a story unless he was happy."

It's not his place to answer now. He wants her to have the last word. It's her right. No-one else's.

"He likes that room. Likes sitting in his own chair. It's a good thing he took it there with him, isn't it, Dei? A good thing that they put it right in front of that big window so he can look out . . . . " She stops, bows her head as if listening for an echo of her own words. "I think it's quite a pleasant room, too."

Spacious and white and warm. Catches all the sun early in the morning.

Dafydd has only just realised that he's bitten his lip hard, so hard. He can taste the blood. The salt-water taste of heartfelt longing. The taste of a tear.

"Yes, Gwyneth, my pet. You're right. It is a pleasant room."

A Penance

It was a round sun, like a plateful of ice. She couldn't cry. Cold, white heat - relentless, pricking her eyes. But she couldn't cry.

I've slept with her, Glen. That's what he said. And called her Glen as if nothing were the matter. Not Glenys. Why not Glenys? Her name full and cold like the sun. I've slept with her, Glenys. That would've sounded better. Wouldn't it? Well, wouldn't it? I've slept with her, Glenys. Marking the distance. Marking the boundaries. But he called her Glen. Like always. Since always. Since they'd been lovers and her hair had been dark too, long enough for her to pile it up on top of her head - back then . . .

I love you, Glen.

Aren't you going to say something? Say something, Glen. She didn't choose to be silent. That's how it happened. The words wouldn't come. They had frozen inside her thoughts. When she looked at him his eyes had filled up and he looked down at his hands. He made it easy for her to stare at him. His shoulders were heavy and the tension was like a grey thread pulling the tiny muscles of his face taut beneath his skin.

He was broken but looked whole, like a dismembered clockwork toy that had been put together again in a hurry. Something invisible, some small important part from inside him, had gone missing.

"I feel almost sorry for you," she said.

He didn't raise his eyes. He didn't move. It was almost as if he hadn't heard her. And his was a cold silence, a blue frostbite in front of her eyes like the small, stark chequered pattern of his shirt.

"Say something, then, Ifor," she said again. She still had her voice, but without spite, without sound. He would have preferred it if she'd behaved differently - if her tongue had been sharp, purging him. He needed to suffer, to do his penance. She knew that. She recognised that in him. But this softness had possessed her and the unexpected tolerance she felt was greater than she was, frightening her and distancing her from her own self. Wouldn't it have been easier for her too had she been able to chastize? Cross-examine him. Hate him.

"I don't expect you to forgive me, Glen."

The room was full of shadows. She felt aware of her shabby cardigan and the old slippers on her feet. The everyday things that never mattered before.

"She's very beautiful, isn't she?" She wasn't asking him. It was on her mind. In her mind. Ifor making love to Gwyneth Cae Aur while she bound him in her smile. He had dipped his hands into the darkness of her hair, watched her eyes fill with stars. Given her his tenderness . . . .

Shall we get married, Glen? Just say yes . . . .

"I'd give anything to have things back the way they were."

"They'll never be the way they were," she said. Somehow there was not enough longing in her voice.

But he had the answer. She wanted to tell him that. He was the one who'd turned away from her with distant eyes. His sentence hung white above them like a naked bulb. Only that there was no light. Everything in the room absorbed the darkness which spread and took hold, like damp. He saw that she was cold.

"Shall I make us a cup of tea, then?"

She accepted his offer by lifting her face towards him. His words too had dried up on his tongue. She still sat there, reluctant to get up and switch on the light. He saw how motionless she'd become and reached out for the light switch.

"No, don't." He froze now. She sensed his uncertainty and softened her voice to a whisper, a pathetic plea instead of the bitter onslaught he'd been yearning for. "Let it be for a little while yet."

She wanted to express the last drops from the remains of the afternoon. She saw now that the white light had melted over the edge of everything. Now the sky was like an empty plate, all tiny cracks.

But it wasn't a Christmas sky. It was December, that was all. In spite of herself her eyes were drawn to the half-open box of decorations in the corner between the window and the fireplace. The tinselled tendrils winked at her like hidden treasure. If it wasn't for the grandchildren they wouldn't bother decorating the house. It was all for the little ones. The tinsel had only returned since Gwion and Huw were born; they bought little golden baubles and Father Christmas candles and remembered again how to celebrate, even if that was only once a year. It didn't matter that the magic evaporated the minute they heard the car start up and draw away from the house.

She'd always liked Christmas. Time after time, she'd be held spellbound by the sound of unaccompanied carols on a cold night and people's breaths rolling transparent from their mouths. And when Gwenno was born on Christmas Eve the perfection of it all had frightened her. She remembered Ifor with his eyes all dewy and everyone's voices like the peal of bells. Ifor bowled over by it all. And Gwenno, gossamer-skinned, in her little white shawl . . . .

Love you so, Glen; love having it all . . . .

"When are they arriving, then?"

She hadn't seen him come back. She was kneeling in front of the box.

"Who?" An empty word. She knew who. Who else was there?

"The boys."

"Sunday."

"Must remember to get the tree . . . . "

She turned to him. He'd slopped tea into the saucers.

"Yes." And she sighed. The civilized generality of their

conversation was stifling her.

"Do you remember that Christmas when Gwenno was three? When she got that little pram and baby doll . . . . "

She stared at him He was looking at the Christmassy box as if willing the memories from within it.

"She was two."

"What . . . . ?"

"Not three. She got a bike when she was three . . . . "

"A red and yellow one."

"With a bell and a basket."

"She carried the doll in that basket after that."

Their eyes met. She was glad he remembered the little things.

"She fell off it, d'you remember?"

"The path was wet."

"It gave me a hell of a turn, seeing her scream out crying. I thought she'd really hurt herself."

"And after all that, she was only worried about the doll falling out of the basket!"

"She was wearing her little pink coat . . . . "

At that her voice broke. It was thick with tears but she refused their solace and jutted out her chin. It was three years since the accident; the road had been wet that night too. That young, gentle policewoman had sat on the edge of their sofa, her line of duty drawn white across her face. Tea getting cold in everyone's cups to the accompaniment of carefully chosen words, the sound of which seemed to douse Glenys's eyes.

"The children are a comfort to us now. And Robin. We're lucky to have him . . . . he's like a son to us . . . . "

She was restless, waiting for those all-too-predictable half-sentences he was so fond of to cease with the sound of his voice. Gwenno had been so like him in her way, and he'd been so quick to encourage her; they both treated life as a game for grown-up children, racing against their dreams, whilst she, Glenys, with her feet on the ground, cleaned the dust fiercely and purposefully from off the furniture as if she feared there would be magic in it.

"She didn't have to be out on the road that night." Each one of her words melted into its own little bitterness; she could taste the middle of each one - they stung the edges of her tongue like sloes. "If she hadn't been up to no good - hadn't been cheating on her husband . . . . "

And it was in what she didn't say that he heard her accusation against him. It was the silence that screamed at him: like father like daughter. Or rather: as the daughter saw fit to behave, so the father followed suit, burying reality under all those daydreams that cluttered his imagination, avoiding the black-and-white truth because dreams were in colour.

"It won't do any good now to pick at old wounds . . . . "

She looked at him, hating that modest ability of his to calm troubled waters.

"You're right," she said to him. "Why pick at old wounds when we've brand new ones to worry at?"

He wasn't going to take the bait. He'd never do anything but bury his head in his own unease and wait for every storm to pass over him. She couldn't stand any more of his silence, the way he would turn away modestly, even politely. She kicked the box of decorations sharply so that it turned over, spewing its entwined contents around her feet.

"You bastard!" she said. Her eyes glinted dangerously. "Bastard. Bastard. Bastard!" Each time she said it her voice became louder and she could feel the wide vowels swelling up in her mouth. She heard the little golden baubles pop beneath the softness of her slippers as if she were treading on beetles.

He still had his back to her. He kept his eyes to himself.

"Well, say something now then, if you can. Say something. You . . . . bastard!"

She insisted on tasting it again, this quick, rounded word that fell between them constantly and sizzled as if she were spitting into a flame. She could see the shivers rippling the line of his shoulders. Even that wasn't enough. She paused, sharpening her words to draw blood:

"Say it, Ifor. Say her name. Gwyneth. Gwyneth. Gwyneth." There was something compelling her to repeat things three times over; it nearly made her laugh, thinking about it. She swallowed hard against the hysteria brimming up in her throat. "I want to hear you say her name. Say you don't care for her now. Say you've forgotten all about Gwyneth Cae Aur and her little-girl-eyes!"

She had hounded him, lost control of herself. Until he turned to face her. It all ebbed away from her like an emptying vein. She'd succeeded, opened his wound; she knew his weaknesses as well as she knew the wrinkles under her own eyes. And she knew he was cursing the images that were now quavering through his mind, water-coloured like a woman's eyes, smelling of spring. It was being unable to forget that tore his breathing; this was his penance and, supposedly, her victory. But knowing that gave her no satisfaction, and it was too late for either of them to take anything back. His eyes shone like wet shells. It wasn't her name written in them.

Damn you, Gwyneth. Damn you for drawing your fingers hesitantly through my senses. Damn you for making me remember how to touch. You're fragile, yes, inside my head, as fragile as tomorrow, the colour of night beyond the curtain's veil. You're my sorrow . . . .

Tell me, Glen - who'll inherit tomorrow?

A Day of Sunshine and Tears

Tricks with light. That's all they were. Coloured bulbs through tissue paper. Dafydd wondered at them; their fake magic was almost beautiful, like a cheap painting of a sunset, its pinkness becoming gaudy as the eye drew nearer.

"First time you've been in a studio, then, is it?"

A pleasant girl. Young. Too young to be so confident. She carried a clipboard. Her clothes were untidily masculine: a loose shirt over her jeans and a pencil behind her ear, like a carpenter. Then again, this sloppiness seemed to suit her and made him feel more uncomfortable in his collar and tie. His lips felt unnaturally greasy with make-up and the skin of his face was tight.

"You're lucky," said the girl. "Being able to write poetry. Have you published many volumes?"

"One or two."

"Gosh, have you really? That's brilliant!"

"Don't you think there's been a mistake here?" he asked.

She smiled quickly at him, uncertain for the first time.

"What's that, then?"

"Well, me wearing the make-up and you with none!"

It was a poor joke but they both laughed because they had

too much time on their hands.

"Someone will attend to you soon," she said then. "To tell you what to do exactly . . . . . "

"Can't you do that?" He was beginning to like her, to like the shyness shining prettily through her confidence.

"No, 'fraid not. Microphones. That's my department, see?" And with a cheeky little smile she finished arranging the little black cable neatly between his shirt and jacket.

It was a strange thing, Dafydd mused. The fleeting intimacy between strangers which made them behave like old friends. The girl instinctively smoothed the collar of his jacket and said, before disappearing for ever:

"There we are. All done. Good luck with the programme!"

Moments. That was all. But he noticed the little gold earrings between the corn-coloured tendrils of her hair and remembered. Looking back didn't hurt any more. The years had stopped laughing at him. Perhaps that's why he thought about Cadi more and more these days. He was growing old, and didn't old age thrive on memories? It had been so long - Cadi meaning the world to him when he was young and reckless. He still insisted upon loving her in the back of his mind where he kept things that no-one else could get hold of.

"Dafydd?" The programme's presenter welcomed him with a professional intelligence. "Meic Gwyn. Call me Meic. Why don't we take five minutes to rehearse our chat . . . . the kind of questions you'll be asked and so forth . . . . " And he proffered his hand.

The coloured lighting melted into itself as Dafydd sat beneath their heat. He felt vulnerable, there within that square of light with nothing but darkness in front of him, imagining a live audience with their eyes shining like rows of beetles.

"Not nervous, I hope? Once we get started you'll forget everything about the audience out there. And don't worry about mistakes - this is a recording. We can cut, edit - no problem!"

Dafydd fidgeted on the square sofa. Everything was square - the cushions, the lamps, the design of the set - everything thrust its sharp angles into his eyes. He listened to his directions with a dry mouth.

" . . . . and then I'll come round to you last, Dafydd. Thought we'd go after the obvious things first - why you write poetry, how you go about it . . . . "

Why? How? Were there any answers? How did one explain the 'going about it' to anyone? Explain the buzz. Words came constantly to itch at his fingertips. Sometimes, against his will, he'd sit at his desk having left some other task unfinished just in order to obey them. Eventually the muscles of his mind would unwind. Never mind now about cutting the lawn or mending the lock on the outhouse door. This is where he wanted to be. Here, putting words together. Filling the virgin pages with the intricate looped tails of his own complexities. He held his fountain-pen tightly between his thumb and forefinger, so that a small ridge formed along his middle finger, just below the underside of his nail. It was almost as if he had no pen, almost as if the ink flowed through the tips of his fingers. Almost as if he were spilling the contents of his own veins onto the white paper . . . .

"We'll talk about the influences upon your work, of course... "

Dafydd raised his eyebrows; they too were heavy, like his lips. Meic Gwyn continued to explain, to say the same thing in so many different ways, his face becoming more and more happy at the sound of his own voice.

"The things that have inspired your poems - experiences, people. Your sister, perhaps. You have a poem here . . . . the relationship between a brother and sister. Your sister, maybe?"

Gwyneth. Was it Gwyneth he described? That's what people wanted to know. Was she the girl in the poem, hiding within her thoughts where words couldn't reach her? Gwyneth, his eternal little sister. She was quieter these days, and the child hidden within her had already seen beyond the magic and tired sooner. He noticed now that her eyes had learnt how to distance themselves so that he was left on the outside sometimes. He couldn't cope with that. Her daydreams affected him in a way he couldn't explain, couldn't fathom. He feared what she omitted to share with him. He feared those pictures in her mind which combed daylight through those watercolour eyes of hers. She always called him Dei nowadays. Dei. Not Deio. Dafydd longed for the sound of the 'o'. And one day she said to him:

"Where's Ifor now, Dei? He went away, didn't he?"

The afternoon lay in transparent slices across the furniture.

"Yes, Gwyn."

She was arranging chrysanthemums in a glass jug, hovering

like a butterfly above each single flower. And even though her memories were as exquisite as kisses she never mentioned his name again.

In a little while, she said: "These never smell of anything." But she looked at Dafydd as she spoke. The simplicity of her mind was all lit up, identifying with his own loss. "Everbody goes away . . . . or dies. And we're still here. It's hard, isn't it, Dei? Living without people . . . . " She caressed the long, rust-coloured petals with her fingertips, and the girl in the poem, only days later, did exactly the same thing.

"The poem about a mother's death is heartrending," said Meic Gwyn. "I'd like us to talk about that as well - the personal experiences, so to speak . . . ." He had too much enthusiasm, and that was sickly too, like the pink lighting. "It's your own personal grief here, of course?"

"Maybe."

"But you lost your mother at an early age. You must have been drawing on experience when you wrote this. It would be most interesting to have an insight into your background too. After all, we must get to know the man, mustn't we, before we can get to know his work?" He'd just been bullshitting about Mallarmé earlier on. Showing off his knowledge. Or rather, his researcher's.

"What background? We all of us have to lose our mothers at some stage."

Dafydd couldn't help his abrupt answers. He had his way of communicating, and a chat-show like this wasn't it.He hadn't chosen this place to vent his grief, hadn't chosen to do it this way with his senses baking in the unyielding light . . . .

He was almost fifteen, too old to admit, even to himself, that he wanted to remain a child. People's words shone neatly in his head like rows of knives: You must look after your little sister now, Dafydd . . . . be strong for your father . . . . No-one bothered to tell him back then that it took a brave person to cry. He couldn't stand being in the same room as other people's voices, in the same room as his father - and Gwyneth. He couldn't look at Gwyneth. The fear widening her already birdlike eyes reminded him of his own terror. He'd stood there a long time at the foot of the bed: his mother's bed, open like a grave. He waited for the silence to move, for the cracks between the shadows to split open and yield something. But nothing came.Only the realisation that he'd never see his mother again. It wasn't yet evening. His body absorbed the nothingness - the twilight crept up on him, making him one with the half-light which divided the room into shadows. He was unable to shiver - he was too cold for that. The cold clung to him like a web, refusing to reach the faraway nerve-endings in his fingertips, his toes. This feeling never left him. This reality. This unwilling communion with his own paralysed soul.

" . . . . then I thought we'd finish off with the love poems - the tenderness, the hope. You never married, either, did you, Dafydd? Dafydd . . . . is everything alright?"

"Fine. Just a bit hot . . . . these lights."

"Of course. We'll take a short break there. Right, everbody, that's enough rehearsal . . . . Dafydd, nip down for a cuppa or something - we'll resume in half an hour!"

It was pleasantly cool in the washroom. Dafydd took off his coat and rolled up his shirtsleeves. The water felt like a blessing; he noticed how that too turned a dirty shade of pink as he washed the make-up off. His mind relaxed to the sound of the running taps. It didn't matter now about the splashes of water over his shirt - the shower of rain he stepped into afterwards made him even wetter. He stood in it with his jacket over his shoulder. A proper sunshine-and-tears day. He regretted having wasted a good half of it sweltering in front of a make-believe sunset.

There was no sign of Dafydd Parry within that half hour. Bloody ill-mannered, somebody said; typical, said another - poets were oddballs, anyway. A shame, thought the girl in the jeans with the gold studs in her ears, even though they found her microphone in the men's toilets, black against the edge of one of the white washbasins, like a cockroach with a tail.

Like the sun itself

Cadi stared into the coolness of the flowers; she hadn't arranged these. They were too much of a display, and their lily-white purity stifled the space they took up in front of the pulpit. When the congregation turned in anticipation to the first notes of the wedding march, she continued to stare straight in front of her. She knew that Angharad would look beautiful; she'd already seen the wedding-dress - an unaccustomed honour for a future mother-in-law. Rather than that, she looked lingeringly at Dylan as if her eyes were trying to swallow back the minutes that were left to her. He turned his head suddenly to catch a glimpse of his wife-to-be and she felt a sharp stab inside her as if her womb were turning over.

Her hat felt new upon her head. She was somehow glad of its newness, of the shadow of the wide brim light but unyielding above her eyes. Eifion stood like a statue beside her; she was aware of his dark suit filling the corner of her eye. They didn't choose to look at each other these days. She preferred that. In the old days he insisted that their eyes met so that he could reproach her without having to say a word.

It had been difficult for him, too - bringing up another man's child. So difficult. Because it wasn't the little boy's fault. And on birthdays and Christmas the Reverend Eifion Rhys made a valiant attempt to make his eyes appear a father's eyes. Wasn't the minister in him enough to conquer the demons inside him, after all? He passed the odd parcel and helped to blow out the last candle while his principles stuck inside his gut like bits of coloured paper.

When Dylan was three years old they'd had a white Christmas. The small boy grabbed his hand and tried to lead him to the window to watch the sky crumble. She lifted her head from her sewing and smiled because of the child. He noticed all of this as if he were looking in on them from the outside. He was that cold. He stared at the white mottling of the fields and pitied himself: he saw a white magic that was really nothing but a lie and could not marvel at it. His wife turned back to the sewing in her lap. There was nothing to intervene upon their awkwardness save for the breathing of the needle through the heavy material. And the child said:

"It's snowing, Dad!"

The stitching stopped. It was as if the snowflakes were falling into the pools of her eyes.

"Yes," he echoed. "It's snowing."

He could have put out his hand to gently ruffle the pale-skinned little boy's hair, could have lifted him up on his arm, maybe, so that he could see better. But she knew that words were all he had and lowered her eyes. Her punishment had been complete a long time ago. But his lukewarm kindness still formed a skin over everything, making sure that she never forgot . . . .

* * * * * * * * * * * * * * * * * *

"I know, Cadi." They both remembered the knell of his words. "I know about you and Dafydd Cae Aur."

It was a controlled kind of disappointment - as if he were reproaching her for spending the money from the missionary boxes. His calculated distance should have given him the upper hand but somehow nothing touched her. She said nothing to defend herself. Nothing surfaced in the stagnant waters of her eyes.

"I won't let you make me a laughing stock, Cadi."

He spoke to her quietly, tenderly almost. She stared at him as if through a dream. He imagined he could smell her adultery, like a sweet, sad perfume. He tried to feel disgust, but could not: his jealousy was more complicated, lying inside his gut like a slow illness. She stood there dumbly, watching him turn her secret over in his white hands. That was worse than feeling their softness afterwards beneath the thin darkness when it all seemed like a ritual as she bowed her head and knelt before him . . . .

* * * * * * * * * * * * * * * * *

Eifion wasn't marrying them. He looked awkward as part of the congregation in someone else's chapel. Cadi sat with her hands folded while the service flowed over her. In God's presence and little grains of dust hovering in a void where the sun hung in white clusters. She thought how cruel this was, this joining of hearts before an audience of hats. Dylan's shoulders were tense; no one but she could have noticed that. They were the same shoulders as those of the seven-year-old Joseph forgetting his lines as the striped dish-towel slipped down over his forehead: that too had been play-acted in front of a chapel congregation, only that time there had been tinsel from the angels' wings falling over everything and the pretend-magic had made things all right. She felt ashamed as her insides froze when Dylan and Angharad exchanged lovers' glances. His childhood rolled like a film through her mind, and behind it all there were the shadows of her own fingers falling accidentally into the light. Hearts were meant to be free . . . .

* * * * * * * * * * * * * * * * *

"You and me, Cadi. We'll go from here - leave it all behind... "

He was so young. All his future in front of him.

"Go home, Dafydd."

He stood there, motionless, refusing to understand. She was afraid now that he'd touch her, afraid of falling between his reckless words. She stepped back, away from him, and saw his eyes bruising.

"Why are you doing this to me, Cadi?"

He mustn't know that this was torture for her. There would be no turning back then. She was older, wasn't she? Knew what was best? She kept her voice even as she placed a distance between them:

"You'll go back to college next month. Forget about me..."

They were so stupid, those last words, undermining everything. She nearly gave in. She fought against the dizzy spell, the nausea threatening to suffocate her. He mustn't know about this either. She gripped the back of the chair in front of her, her knuckles whitening - her pregnancy had begun to reproach her days ago. She was determined not to ruin his life. It wasn't his fault that she was lonely and vulnerable and that her marriage was cold. She'd give Dafydd Cae Aur his future back. The idea of sacrificing something made her feel pure, and kept the pain at bay for a little while longer. She closed her heart around the child in her womb and depended upon it; this new relationship was already unconditional. This love didn't come from the outside world. For once she was glad to be able to be selfish enough to keep at least one gift for herself . . . .

* * * * * * * * * * * * * * * * * *

"He's a credit to you, Cadi."

Because the tenderness in those words was so unexpected she couldn't draw comfort from it. But his had been a valid attempt to sound kind and that touched something within her. Her voice cracked and betrayed her:

"You did your bit too." Her acknowledgement of that fact was an effort too. She sounded so polite. This was a careful conversation with both of them following its path like children lost in a wood.

"It was never any fault of Dylan's. What good would it

have done to take it out on him . . . . "

"It's me you took it out on."

Eifion had chosen his words carelessly and she was unable to forgive. It was so easy to answer abruptly having had bitterness sustain her so long. But something akin to tiredness relaxed the muscles of his face and crept into his eyes. For a moment she almost regretted it. He spoke with more restraint:

"I hadn't intended to reproach you . . . . " That sentence dried up. "There's no need for this now. We don't want to spoil today for them . . . . "

"No."

Gusts of laughter and confetti reached the edge of their conversation. The photographer looked anxiously in their direction. He offered her an excuse to escape by waving at her and pointing at the camera. But Cadi stood still. She didn't want to go.

"You were a good father to him, fair play to you." Now her voice seemed about to split open. "You didn't have to do it." At last, she looked at him. "You had a choice, you know."

"No, Cadi." Softly, softly. His words soft. "Not really."

The heat of the sun opened out above them like a fist unclenching.

"It was because of him I got up every day," she said, without malice.

He watched her as she remembered her morning routine. Straightening her bedcover neatly across the awkwardness. How many times had he lain awake on the other side of the wall, letting her busy sounds torture him? He would imagine her straightening the signs of one person's sleep in a double bed, smoothing the modest creases out of a clean pillow.

"You don't know how often I yearned for him to have been my son," he said.

Cadi could smell flowers. He noticed her opening her eyes wide as if she were trying to fill them with a picture that was too beautiful; he remembered how unusual, how changeable their blueness was.

"But he is your son," she said, too lightly. "You brought him up, after all . . . . "

The fickleness in her eyes wavered through her voice too, and he knew that she was trying to thank him. But her perfume was close to him, warm and familiar. He embraced the past, looking through his own nostalgia so that he could see her better.

"They want us to go over," he said. "For the photographs."

"Yes." For the album that would be bound in white like the covers of her memories. The sun put its hand on her shoulder, warm as a promise.

"Shall we go over and join them, then?" He offered her his arm.

The light touch of her fingers upon his sleeve was shy like the sun itself.

Between a White Night
and Daybreak

You'll stay overnight on the outskirts. A pub providing bed and breakfast. Just the thing. A pint and an open fire and no-one to recognise you. You'll be full of doubts. Your brain overflowing with them. But there will be no turning back. Not now. Not with her having told you. At last.

Soon it'll be the following morning, that 'day after' that you'd been mulling over when last night began to stifle you. Daylight unfolding in front of your eyes and the smell of your fried breakfast being prepared somewhere, mixing with the smell of this place which has a faint whiff of stale beer tainting its breath.

"Sleep well?"

"Fine, thanks." Why tell the whole truth? A cold, clean bed and your mind slipping reluctantly between the sheets. Last night there was a round moon like a spectacle lens, and a smattering of mist bleaching the darkness and dimming the stars until they became cloudy like old people's eyes. A white night. You knew then that tomorrow would be inevitable and that it would swallow you, body and soul. Tomorrow you would be an unexpected guest. You should have telephoned. Sent a note. But you were too much of a coward. Afraid of the response. Too late now. You'll imagine a door being shut in your face . . . .

You'll see a strangeness about a pub at daybreak. Only your car in the car park outside. Today will be your fortieth birthday. You'll feel a lopsided smile creasing your insides. If you and Angharad had still been together there'd have been a fair bit of celebrating. Organising parties had been one of her fortes . . . . The smile will turn on itself, leaving a round mark in your gut. The divorce wasn't unexpected: it touched you like a distant bereavement, playing on your mind without making you cry. You'd been living apart for months before receiving your letters through the post. Absolute. Neat and final. It's days like this that will knock you back down again - days with headings above them, days that were once dates circled in red.

You'll think of your mother upon this morning forty years ago. You were a daybreak baby. Those were her words to you. Often. You'll imagine again the joy on her face, her firstborn arriving with the first light of day and the dawn cleaner because of it, lifting its canopy over the pinkness of it all. You've always been painfully close to your mother. That's why today will be special. You'll be doing this today for her sake too. In memory. Because of all that happened. You'll interrupt the flow of your own thoughts by starting the car engine.

You'll have the address. On paper and in your memory. A pretty name shining in your head. But the directions. They'll be more of a puzzle, a hedgerowed network of country lanes and grey gates with no names on them. You'll linger awhile when you get to the village. There will only be ten minutes or so of the journey left. You'll leave the car and walk around a bit. Your mother has mentioned this place so often over the years. The little grey chapel on the slope, the row of tall houses with a dark dignity about them, looking out towards the sea. It'll be like walking in between the pages of a story and getting a buzz out of knowing that it wasn't make-believe after all. Having clambered up the steep slope with its shoulder leaning towards the salty smells of the beach you'll discover the sea for yourself. That will be disappointing; so far away - you won't see much apart from long stretches of sand and a seagull or two like careless gobbets spat between the eyes of the grey pools. You'll breathe in the stillness. This infinite loneliness will open out in front of you, and the vastness will entice you to free your senses. The grey mysticism of this scene says you've been here before. You'll feel the morning cold grip the nape of your neck while the landscape behind you flinches beneath a wet hoar-frost. This will do you good. All this. This waiting. Standing here to stare. You'll be doing the right thing. You wanted to belong.

You won't feel the damp in your shoes until you get back to the car. It's as if the morning itself insists upon clinging to the soles of your feet. You'll feel strangely small, and the day too big around you; your mind will be brimming over with the vastness of the beach. Two, three miles beyond the village you'll take a left turn off the main road. This road will be so narrow in places that there will be no room for two cars to pass each other. You'll be eternally grateful that no other vehicle came towards you. And yet, the loneliness of these places will seem oppressive. The dark, winding, wooded roads. It will seem as though all the secrets of creation have been woven into the hedgerows.

You'll try and begin to remember. Stories. Legends. Directions. An old water-mill. A sharp bend in the road. Past a couple of cottages, a kissing gate and a marsh. You'll arrive too soon somehow. You'll be there before having had time to prepare yourself, your car nosing its way hesitantly like a living thing between the two gateposts at the entrance. There won't be a nameplate. Nothing to give it away. Only the clean, whitewashed walls making the windows of the house appear darker like sunglasses hiding the soul within. This will be Cae Aur.

You'll stand for a long time on the doorstep. So long that you'll give a start when its finally opened to you.

"Yes?" A tall, thin, dark-eyed man, his hair almost white. His face will be painfully familiar even though he too knows that this is the first time you've ever met.

"I'm not sure if I've come to the right place . . . ." Even though you know full well that you have. You'll be playing for time. Praying for confidence. Hoping for his co-operation. The moments will pile up on top of each other. The thin face will stare at you without expression, waiting for an explanation.

"I'm looking for Dafydd Parry."

The black eyes will not move. They won't betray a thing.

"Who are you, then?"

"The name's Dylan Rhys." You'll offer your hand. "Cadi's son." And retract your hand just as quickly. You'll see his eyes shimmer then as if he's shuffling through well-thumbed pages in his mind.

"You're Cadi Rhys's son." It won't be a question but a stunned echo, the words oddly soft as their tails intertwine.

"Yes."

"How is she these days?"

The pain will stretch across your eyes and remain there for some moments in a straight line like a brushstroke. Then you'll say to him:

"She died . . . . four months ago . . . . " You'll clear your throat and the awkwardness threatens to choke you.

"I'm very sorry to hear that." Dafydd Parry has always been one to speak quietly. His words will sound more tender perhaps than they're actually meant to be. Your determination will waver at that. The nape of your neck will feel cold.

"I'm sorry too - for troubling you - coming here like this . . . . I should never have . . . . "

"Come into the house."

The unexpected invitation will hover between you. You'll see that he'll have turned back into the house expecting you to follow his words. The rooms will be small, much smaller than you'd anticipated. You'll find everything clean and neat; he'll lead you into a living room with too much furniture in it. It will be obvious that it's also a dining-room; there will be a table with a cloth on it under the window upon which will be a sugar bowl and a cooling teapot. The fire will be just starting to take hold, and a thin worm-like flame will be tickling the fresh lumps of coal. You'll see a thin woman sitting in front of it. You'll guess that she's about fifty. But you already have an inkling of her age. She'll look shivery with the room not yet warmed. Her eyes will wander restlessly over you with the sulky, irritable look of a tired child. Her grey hair will be smooth, cut in a straight, classic bobbed style and just reaching her shoulders. She was once a stunning girl; you'll see how effortless her beauty is still, something ageless that no layer of make-up could ever have enhanced. You'll realise that you've stared too long at her: you'll admire the perfection of her cheekbones as if appreciating a piece of fine art. Your mother has mentioned her too. Described her so carefully to you that her pale beauty does not surprise you.

"Gwyneth? There's a young man called to see us."

Her brother will touch her arm lightly, using his words to draw her into what will happen next. Us. To see us. That will lock their eyes together for an instant, keeping you a stranger on the outside of things. This won't disturb her at all. You'll see her play with a lock of her hair and look back into the fire where a curl of blue smoke is both tightening and slackening like a slip-knot.

"Sit down." He'll offer you a small armchair. The woman will stare at you silently and then smile shyly and suddenly, offering you her eyes as if she's sharing sweets. You'll sit there awkwardly in your low chair and realise that you've just recognised your own face as you look at Dafydd Parry. The similarity between you is striking and gives you an odd boost of confidence . . . .

"I know this will come as a bit of a shock to you . . . . "

You'll see Dafydd Parry raise his eyebrows slightly but his face will remain pale and expressionless.

" . . . . to be honest, I don't really know where to begin..."

"You don't need to, my boy . . . . "

And then it'll be your turn to look surprised. This quiet man with his sudden sentences will have addressed you with an irreversible familiarity before reaching himself a high chair from in front of the table and drawing it nearer the fire. He's used to sitting like this, on a hard chair, straight-backed, higher up than everyone else. You'll notice how his eyes swiftly comb over the small hearth before looking directly into your face. It will be as if he's just drawn sustenance from the four walls of his own kitchen. And that's when you'll realise that you won't need to tell him. He'll know. Only by looking at you. Your face will be enough, your colouring and your quiet determination. But your eyes. Your eyes are different. They're blue. But he can't fail to recognise them. To recognise that pale blue that looks as if it's faded in the wash. He'll remember the blueness. As he'll remember that sudden hill mist when she held on to him ; when they waited together for the woolly dampness to crumble above them until they could see the mountainside between tendrils of cloud before embracing each other. And then he'll remember a damp August evening forty years ago when the hedgerows were dripping with rain . . . .

"You have your mother's eyes." He'll be talking partly to you, partly to himself. Saying what matters with his face.

"Is he Cadi's boy?"

When she speaks you'll both look in the direction of her sudden words and watch her shrink back into her shell of shyness like a child frightened by its own boldness in the presence of adults. But Dafydd's tenderness will touch you as he leans forward and takes hold of her hand so that he may entice her eyes back into your conversation. You'll see a glow beneath her cheekbones as this retrieves her awkward dignity.

"Yes, Gwyneth. Cadi's boy." He'll keep a hold of her hand.

"I remember Cadi."

"Yes . . . ."

"You and Cadi." You'll hear the beat of your own heart racing against the ticking of the clock while the past remains still like old dust trapped within the kitchen walls. He and Cadi. Together. Apart. An ageing bachelor having chosen to shroud his soul with his longing for a lost love. And Gwyneth will still be talking into a void, still sweeping yesterday into the picture and it'll be damp and wizened and brittle all at once, short-lived bits and pieces like the dead leaves of her own words.

"Remember Cadi . . . . remember the storm . . . . "

You won't understand. You won't be allowed to see the faraway guilt in his eyes because he'll get up and pretend to stare out of the window; he'll turn his back for a while with his left hand kneading his right hand, the hand that held onto Gwyneth's just now. How can you understand without knowing about the night of the storm when he went to her and made love to her? And conceived you, neatly underlining that last farewell; you were there being formed between their mingling breath and he suspected nothing.

You'll find that he won't ask you much. He's always been that way, one to bow his head and accept things. Modesty runs in the family. It's that same modesty that dampens your confidence at times. You inherited that impulsive streak of yours from your mother. That instinctive curiosity which makes you want to give each day a good shake to see what'll fall out. The passion. It's a good thing. Your father's level-headedness is in there somewhere and that's a good thing too. Because you need both of these things.

I don't know what will happen to you afterwards. That's more than anyone can say. But I know you'll go and find him. You'll find each other. You'll go through your own turmoil first, mind you, before that happens. Before you arrive at Cae Aur with your hopes tucked into a tight little parcel under your arm. And when he tells you - about thunderstorms and mist and duty and guilt, about loving and losing and counting the hours between a white night and daybreak - you'll understand, identify with the longing in those unfinished sentences brimming over his thoughts . . . .

You'll remember when you were young, too, sleeping through the night because the day tired you out. And that morning when you woke up older than your age and asked who you were. From the moment you asked, you knew that every tomorrow would be a mirror in which you would search for your own face and recognise it for the first time.

You'll go looking for your father before the dew rises. What will it matter? You waited a long time. Don't be afraid; you have your mother's eyes. You can offer him back yesterday and the hoar-frost will be damp beneath your shoes too.